*To Maria, who is never afraid to
dance to the beat of her own drum.*
~ Dave

Text and Illustrations © 2013 Dave Whamond

Owlkids Books acknowledges the financial support of the Canada Council for the Arts, the Ontario Arts Council, the Government of Canada through the Canada Book Fund (CBF) and the Government of Ontario through the Ontario Media Development Corporation's Book Initiative for our publishing activities.

Published in Canada by
Owlkids Books Inc.
10 Lower Spadina Avenue
Toronto, ON M5V 2Z2

Published in the United States by
Owlkids Books Inc.
1700 Fourth Street
Berkeley, CA 94710

Library and Archives Canada Cataloguing in Publication

Whamond, Dave
    Oddrey and the new kid / Dave Whamond.

ISBN 978-1-926973-90-6

    I. Title.

PS8645.H34O34 2013   jC813'.6   C2012-908522-7

Library of Congress Control Number: 2013930983

Design: Barb Kelly

Manufactured in Shenzhen, China, in February 2013, by C&C Joint Printing Co., (Guangdong) Ltd. Job #HN0924

A   B   C   D   E   F

Publisher of Chirp, chickaDEE and OWL
www.owlkidsbooks.com

Oddrey

and the New Kid

Written and illustrated by

DAVE WHAMOND

Owl
kids

Oddrey was always a bit different from the other kids at school.

Her teacher said lessons were never boring with Oddrey in the classroom.

Her classmates said Oddrey always seemed to stand out.

Her dog Ernie said, "Awooo!"

Oddrey loved spending time with her friends.
They appreciated her unique style, and she
encouraged them to reach for the sky.

When Oddrey's teacher introduced a new student to the class, Oddrey was excited. She was sure they would be the best of friends.

Oddrey and her classmates thought the new girl was fascinating and mysterious. Her name was Maybelline, and she had travelled to the four corners of the earth with her dad.

Maybelline was good at inventing fun games at recess.
And she very quickly took on the role of leader.

As time went on, Oddrey began to suspect that
Maybelline might be telling tall tales.

But the kids at school just couldn't get enough
of Maybelline's stories.

And one day, on a class field trip to the zoo,
Oddrey decided that she had had enough.

"Is that story really true?" she asked Maybelline.

"Of course it's true," Maybelline replied. "My dad and I have adventures all the time. In fact, see that monkey over there? I'm going to rescue it!"

Before Oddrey and her classmates even realized what was happening, Maybelline had grabbed a loose vine and was swooping down into the monkey enclosure!

Oddrey could see that Maybelline was in trouble. She figured it was up to her to help.

The two girls managed to save the monkey, but they were now in an even bigger jam.

After thinking for a minute, Oddrey grabbed Maybelline's hand and jumped on to the monkey's tire swing.

"That was my best adventure yet," said Maybelline.

Oddrey had to agree.